Sports Illustrated KIDS

LEGENDS IN THE MAKING

BASEBALL LEGENDS IN THE MAKING

BY MARTY GITLIN

CAPSTONE PRESS
a capstone imprint

Sports Illustrated Kids Legends in the Making are published by Capstone Press,
1710 Roe Crest Drive, North Mankato, Minnesota 56003
www.capstonepub.com

Library of Congress Cataloging-in-Publication Data
Gitlin, Marty.
  Baseball legends in the making / by Marty Gitlin.
     pages cm.—(Sports illustrated kids. Legends in the making)
  Includes index.
  ISBN 978-1-4765-4062-7 (library binding)
  ISBN 978-1-4765-5188-3 (paperback)
1. Baseball players—Biography—Juvenile literature. I. Title.
  GV865.A1G53 2013
  796.357092'2—dc23   2013032770

Editorial Credits
Anthony Wacholtz, editor; Ted Williams, set designer; Terri Poburka, designer;
    Eric Gohl, media researcher; Jennifer Walker, production specialist

Photo Credits
Newscom: EPA/Erik S. Lesser, 20; Shutterstock: Alex Staroseltsev, 1; *Sports Illustrated:*
Al Tielemans, cover (bottom left), 14, 14–15 (bkg), 22–23 (bkg), 25, 29, 31 (bottom),
Bob Rosato, 20–21 (bkg), Damian Strohmeyer, 10–11 (bkg), 12–13 (bkg), 19, David E.
Klutho, 16, 23, 24–25 (bkg), 26–27 (bkg), John Biever, cover (bottom right), 8, 11, 16–17
(bkg), 26, 28–29 (bkg), John W. McDonough, 18–19 (bkg), Robert Beck, cover (top), 4,
4–5 (bkg), 6–7 (bkg), 8–9 (bkg), 12, 30, Simon Bruty, 6, 31 (top)

Design Elements
Shutterstock

Printed in the United States of America in Stevens Point, Wisconsin.
092013   007768WZS14

TABLE OF CONTENTS

Some athletes in Major League Baseball (MLB) create excitement throughout the league. Their talents and personalities bring new fans to the sport. These players have established themselves as legends in the making.

CARLOS GONZALEZ

POSITION:
OUTFIELDER

HEIGHT:	**WEIGHT:**
6 FEET 1 INCH (185 CM)	**220 POUNDS (100 KG)**

HIGH SCHOOL:
LICIO UDON PEREZ MARACAIBO, VENEZUELA

MLB TEAM:
COLORADO ROCKIES

Carlos Gonzalez does everything well on the baseball field. His combination of speed and power makes him a dangerous part of the Colorado lineup.

"CarGo" began his major league career with the Oakland Athletics in 2008 and was traded to the Rockies later that year. In 2010 he led the National League with 197 hits, a .336 batting average, and 351 total bases. He hit 34 home runs, stole a career-high 26 bases, and finished third in the Most Valuable Player voting that season.

Gonzalez continued to shine in 2012. He stole 20 bases and won a **Gold Glove Award** for his amazing play in the outfield. Although he was injured for part of 2013, he still hit 26 home runs and stole 21 bases.

⟿ Did You Know

Gonzalez made his major league debut with the Oakland Athletics on May 30, 2008, his mother's birthday. She traveled from Venezuela to watch him play.

GOLD GLOVE AWARD—an annual award given to the best defensive player at each position

DEBUT—a player's first game

CLAYTON KERSHAW

POSITION:
STARTING PITCHER

HEIGHT:	WEIGHT:
6 FEET 3 INCHES	220 POUNDS
(191 CM)	(100 KG)

HIGH SCHOOL:
HIGHLAND PARK
DALLAS, TEXAS

// MLB TEAM:
LOS ANGELES DODGERS

Clayton Kershaw is a flame-throwing left-hander and perhaps the best young pitcher in the game. He spent just one full season in the **minor leagues** before making his debut with the Dodgers in 2008. He displayed his talents by yielding just 119 hits in 171 innings in 2009. He also averaged more than one strikeout per inning that season.

Kershaw blossomed into a star in 2011. He led the National League in wins (21), earned run average (2.28), and strikeouts (248). It is no wonder that he won the **Cy Young Award** that year. In 2012 he led the league with a 2.53 ERA and placed second in the Cy Young voting. Kershaw only got better in 2013. He went 16-9 with 232 strikeouts and a league-best 1.83 ERA. He led the Dodgers to the National League Championship Series for the first time since 2009.

⤷ Did You Know

Kershaw and his wife, Ellen, travel to Africa to help children in need. Kershaw won the 2012 Roberto Clemente Award for his charity work.

MINOR LEAGUES—a level of professional baseball below the major leagues

CY YOUNG AWARD—an award given every season to the best pitcher in each league

BUSTER POSEY

POSITION:

CATCHER

HEIGHT:	WEIGHT:
6 FEET 1 INCH (185 CM)	220 POUNDS (100 KG)

COLLEGE:
FLORIDA STATE UNIVERSITY

MLB TEAM:
SAN FRANCISCO GIANTS

Buster Posey is one of the best catchers in baseball. He made an immediate impact with the San Francisco Giants when he became a starter in 2010. He batted .305 and struck out just 55 times all season. He won National League Rookie of the Year honors.

Posey overcame a season-ending ankle injury in 2011 to bounce back in 2012. He led the National League with a .336 batting average. He hit 24 home runs and led all major league catchers with 103 runs batted in. He belted a home run in Game 4 of the World Series to help the Giants complete a four-game **sweep** of the Detroit Tigers. It came as no surprise when he was voted the National League MVP. In 2013 he earned his second consecutive spot on the NL All-Star team.

⇨ Did You Know

Posey plays the game with confidence, but baseball can be a game of nerves. Posey admits that he was most nervous while catching the perfect game thrown by teammate Matt Cain in June 2012. Posey contributed two hits and a run scored in the 10-0 defeat of the Houston Astros.

SWEEP—when a team wins all of the games in a series

David Price is one of the most consistent and talented pitchers in the sport. His pinpoint control frustrates hitters. He was snagged by Tampa Bay with the first overall pick in the 2007 **amateur draft**. He blossomed in 2010 with an impressive 19-6 record and 2.72 earned run average that led the American League.

Price placed second in the Cy Young Award voting in 2010, but he captured the honor in 2012. He earned a sparkling 20-5 record that season and led the American League with a 2.56 ERA. He was chosen to be on the AL All-Star team every season from 2010 to 2012 while averaging nearly one strikeout per inning. In 2013 he threw four complete games, tying Chris Sale of the White Sox for most in the American League.

⇨ Did You Know

Price was an Atlanta Braves fan growing up in Tennessee. His favorite player was outfielder David Justice. Price was 10 years old in 1995 when Justice helped the Braves to a World Series win over the Cleveland Indians.

AMATEUR DRAFT—an event in which major league organizations select the best high school and college players

DAVID PRICE

POSITION:
STARTING PITCHER

HEIGHT:	WEIGHT:
6 FEET 6 INCHES (198 CM)	220 POUNDS (100 KG)

COLLEGE:
VANDERBILT UNIVERSITY

// MLB TEAM:
TAMPA BAY RAYS

FELIX HERNANDEZ

POSITION:
STARTING PITCHER

HEIGHT:	WEIGHT:
6 FEET 3 INCHES (191 CM)	230 POUNDS (104 KG)

HIGH SCHOOL:
U.E. JOSE AUSTRE
VALENCIA, VENEZUELA

MLB TEAM:
SEATTLE MARINERS

There is a reason Felix Hernandez earned the nickname "King Felix." He is perhaps the most dominant right-hander in baseball. He took the sport by storm in 2005 at the age of 19. In his first three starts with the Seattle Mariners, he gave up just two earned runs and won twice. He picked up steam in 2009. That year he led the American League with 19 victories and recorded a brilliant 2.49 earned run average. He came in second in the 2009 AL Cy Young voting.

Hernandez has overcome poor run support to earn recognition for his work. Despite a 13-12 record in 2010, he won the AL Cy Young Award with a 2.27 ERA. He also hurled the first **perfect game** in Mariners history on August 15, 2012. He has earned a spot on the AL All-Star team four times. The 2013 season marked the fifth consecutive year Hernandez racked up more than 200 strikeouts.

⇨ Did You Know

Hernandez could throw a baseball at 90 miles per hour by age 14.

PERFECT GAME—a game in which a pitcher doesn't allow any batters to reach base

ANDREW McCUTCHEN

POSITION:

OUTFIELDER

HEIGHT:	WEIGHT:
5 FEET 10 INCHES (178 CM)	185 POUNDS (84 KG)

HIGH SCHOOL:

FORT MEADE
FORT MEADE, FLORIDA

// MLB TEAM:
PITTSBURGH PIRATES

Andrew McCutchen has emerged as one of the most exciting players in the game. He has been destroying National League pitching and burning up the base paths since his debut with the Pirates in 2009. He finished fourth in the Rookie of the Year voting with a .286 batting average and 22 stolen bases.

McCutchen has improved every season. He clubbed 35 doubles in 2010 and earned a trip to the All-Star Game the next year. He exploded into greatness in 2012, recording career highs in hits (194), runs (107), home runs (31), and RBIs (96). He also stole 20 bases. Some fans thought he should have won the National League MVP award, but he finished third in the voting.

McCutchen continued his all-around stellar play in 2013 and was named an NL All-Star for the third time. He helped the Pirates to their first postseason appearance in 21 years.

⤷ Did You Know

McCutchen smashed three home runs in one game against Washington on August 2, 2009. His father, Lorenzo, and mother, Petrina, were in the stands celebrating their wedding anniversary.

AROLDIS
CHAPMAN

POSITION:

RELIEF PITCHER

HEIGHT:	WEIGHT:
6 FEET 4 INCHES (193 CM)	205 POUNDS (93 KG)

MLB TEAM:
CINCINNATI REDS

No pitcher in Major League Baseball fires a fastball like Aroldis Chapman. In fact, he has a record-setting fastball. In September 2010, his first season with Cincinnati, he tossed the fastest pitch recorded in major league history. His fastball to San Diego batter Tony Gwynn Jr. was clocked at 105 miles per hour.

Chapman has since established himself as one of the best strikeout pitchers in the sport. In 2011 he fanned 71 batters and surrendered just 24 hits in 50 innings. He emerged as the Reds' **closer** the following year and earned 38 saves. He recorded an amazing 122 strikeouts in 71.2 innings in 2012. The next season he again earned 38 saves while striking out 112 batters over 63.2 innings.

Did You Know

Chapman began his baseball career in Cuba as a first baseman before converting to a pitcher. He struck out more than a batter an inning for the Cuban National Team from 2006 to 2009.

CLOSER—a pitcher brought in during the late innings, usually to save the game

Giancarlo Stanton can smash a baseball out of the park. He is among the most feared sluggers in the game. He made an immediate impact as a 20-year-old rookie in 2010 with 22 home runs in just 359 at bats.

Stanton continued to clobber major league pitching the following seasons. He smashed 34 home runs in 2011 and led the National League with a .608 **slugging percentage** in 2012. He recorded career-highs with a .290 batting average and 37 home runs that season to earn his first All-Star Game appearance. Stanton missed more than a month in 2013 because of a hamstring injury, but he still managed to blast 24 home runs.

⤷ Did You Know

Stanton hit the longest home run of the 2012 MLB season. He crushed a pitch from Colorado Rockies pitcher Josh Roenicke on August 17 at Coors Field. The ball carried 494 feet (151 meters).

SLUGGING PERCENTAGE—a statistic that divides a player's home runs, triples, doubles, and singles by the number of at bats

GIANCARLO
STANTON

POSITION:

OUTFIELDER

HEIGHT:	**WEIGHT:**
6 FEET 6 INCHES (198 CM)	240 POUNDS (109 KG)

HIGH SCHOOL:
NOTRE DAME
SHERMAN OAKS, CALIFORNIA

MLB TEAM:
MIAMI MARLINS

CRAIG
KIMBREL

POSITION:

RELIEF PITCHER

HEIGHT:	WEIGHT:
5 FEET 11 INCHES (180 CM)	205 POUNDS (93 KG)

COLLEGE:
WALLACE STATE
COMMUNITY COLLEGE

MLB TEAM:
ATLANTA BRAVES

Craig Kimbrel wasted no time proving himself as one of the most dominant pitchers in baseball. He arrived in Atlanta in 2010. He gave up only one earned run in 21 games that season. He struck out 40 batters in just 20.2 innings.

The Braves placed Kimbrel in the closer role in 2011, where he continued to dominate. He led the National League with 46 saves, and he struck out 127 batters in 77 innings. He struck out half the batters he faced in 2012 while again leading the NL in saves with 42. He held batters to a .126 batting average and helped the Braves into the **playoffs**. He topped the majors in 2013 with 50 saves and became an All-Star for the third time.

⤵ Did You Know

Kimbrel dropped a stack of sheet rock on his foot while working a summer job in 2006. He could not put weight on his foot, so he began throwing pitches from his knees in practice to improve his strength.

PLAYOFFS—a series of games played after the regular season to determine a champion

Tampa Bay was one of the worst franchises in baseball until Evan Longoria joined the team in 2008. He led the Rays to their first World Series that season by slugging 27 home runs and winning AL Rookie of the Year.

Longoria was just warming up. In 2009 he blasted 33 home runs and tallied 113 RBIs. He continued to roll in 2010 with 104 RBIs and a career-best .294 batting average. He showed his defensive side by winning his second Gold Glove Award for his abilities at third base. In 2011 Longoria showed he could come through in the clutch. He slammed two home runs in the final game of the 2011 regular season to propel the Rays into the playoffs. He was slowed by a back injury in 2012, but he returned to form in 2013. That year he slugged 32 home runs and 39 doubles.

⤳ Did You Know

Longoria didn't receive any college baseball offers because scouts thought he was too skinny. He worked out and gained 40 pounds, earning a shot at Long Beach State. He didn't disappoint—he won Big West Conference Player of the Year honors in 2006.

EVAN LONGORIA

POSITION:

THIRD BASEMAN

HEIGHT:	WEIGHT:
6 FEET 2 INCHES (188 CM)	210 POUNDS (95 KG)

COLLEGE:
LONG BEACH STATE UNIVERSITY

// MLB TEAM:
TAMPA BAY RAYS

23

Gio Gonzalez took a bit longer to grow into greatness than did some of the other young stars of baseball. He entered the league in 2008 but didn't truly hit his stride until 2010. That year he earned an American League All-Star spot with the Oakland Athletics while compiling a 15-9 record and 3.23 ERA.

Gonzalez enjoyed another strong year with the Athletics in 2011 before a trade landed him in Washington. He went from good to sensational in 2012 with the Nationals. He won 21 games to lead the majors and help the Nationals secure their first playoff berth. Gonzalez struck out more than a batter per inning in the process. He continued to mow down hitters in 2013, striking out 192 batters in 195.2 innings.

⇨ Did You Know

Gonzalez began a charity in 2012 called Giving Individuals Opportunities (GIO). As part of his charity work, he spoke to students in Washington, D.C., about bullying. He also worked with young cancer patients in Boston.

GIO
GONZALEZ

POSITION:
STARTING PITCHER

HEIGHT:	WEIGHT:
6 FEET (183 CM)	200 POUNDS (91 KG)

HIGH SCHOOL:
MONSIGNOR EDWARD PACE
MIAMI, FLORIDA

MLB TEAMS:
OAKLAND ATHLETICS, WASHINGTON NATIONALS

MIGUEL CABRERA

POSITION:
THIRD BASEMAN

HEIGHT:	WEIGHT:
6 FEET 4 INCHES (193 CM)	240 POUNDS (109 KG)

HIGH SCHOOL:
MARACAY
MARACAY, VENEZUELA

MLB TEAMS:
FLORIDA MARLINS, DETROIT TIGERS

Miguel Cabrera is widely considered the greatest hitter in the game. He emerged as a star with the Florida Marlins, recording at least 26 home runs and 112 RBIs every year from 2004 to 2007. It was no surprise that he earned a spot on the NL All-Star team each of those seasons.

Cabrera continued his amazing hitting after being traded to the Detroit Tigers in 2007. He led the American League with 37 home runs in 2008 and 126 RBIs in 2010. He earned the major league batting title the following season.

Cabrera achieved an amazing feat in 2012. He won the first **Triple Crown** in Major League Baseball since 1967. He had a .330 batting average, a career-high 44 home runs, and 139 RBIs. He continued to shine in 2013, when he hit a league-best .348. He came in second in the league with 44 home runs and 137 RBIs.

Did You Know

Cabrera's teammates nominated him for the Roberto Clemente Award in 2012.

TRIPLE CROWN—awarded to a player who leads his league in batting average, home runs, and RBIs in the same season

Jay Bruce has been a streak hitter since joining the Reds in 2008. But he was hot often enough that year to place fifth in the NL Rookie of the Year voting. He slugged 21 home runs in 2008 and continued to increase his production.

Bruce exploded for 32 home runs and 97 RBIs in 2011 to secure a spot on the NL All-Star team. In 2012 he earned career highs with 34 home runs, 35 doubles, and 99 RBIs. He placed among the leaders in the NL Most Valuable Player voting. He went on an amazing tear in June 2013 with eight home runs in a nine-game stretch. He finished the season with career highs in hits (164), doubles (43), and RBIs (109).

⇨ Did You Know

Bruce swung a sizzling bat when he was promoted from the minor leagues to Cincinnati in May 2008. In his first six games, he batted .577 with 12 runs, three doubles, three home runs, seven RBIs, and two stolen bases.

JAY
BRUCE

POSITION:
OUTFIELDER

HEIGHT:	WEIGHT:
6 FEET 3 INCHES (191 CM)	215 POUNDS (98 KG)

HIGH SCHOOL:
WEST BROOK
BEAUMONT, TEXAS

MLB TEAM:
CINCINNATI REDS

RISING STARS

BRYCE HARPER

The top pick in the 2010 draft raced through the Washington Nationals' minor league system. He began the 2012 season in the major leagues. He was named NL Rookie of the Year by batting .270 with 22 home runs and 18 stolen bases. He continued his hot hitting in 2013 and earned a second All-Star appearance.

YASIEL PUIG ↳

Puig burst onto the MLB scene with the Los Angeles Dodgers in 2013. He hit four home runs in his first five games and ended the season with a .319 batting average.

CHRIS SALE

The Chicago White Sox took the left-hander with a blazing fastball in the first round of the 2010 draft. He dominated hitters as a relief pitcher his first two seasons. As a starting pitcher in 2012, he had a 17-8 record and struck out 192 batters in 192 innings pitched. The next season he struck out 226 batters, which was fourth best in the majors.

STEPHEN STRASBURG

Strasburg was the first overall pick of the 2009 draft. He struck out 14 Pittsburgh Pirates in just seven innings on June 8, 2010, in an amazing major league debut with the Washington Nationals. He earned a spot on the NL All-Star team in 2012. In 2013 he struck out 191 batters in 183 innings.

MIKE TROUT

The 2012 American League Rookie of the Year led the league with 129 runs and 49 stolen bases. He nearly won the MVP award for his efforts. Trout also blasted 30 home runs and 27 doubles. The next season he hit 27 home runs and 39 doubles while showing patience at the plate with 110 walks.

MANNY MACHADO

Machado has blossomed into one of the best young third basemen in the sport. He helped the Baltimore Orioles into the playoffs in 2012 with his powerful swing and reliable glove. In 2013 Machado was second in the majors with 51 doubles and earned a spot on the AL All-Star team.

READ MORE

Jacobs, Greg. *The Everything Kids' Baseball Book.*
Avon, Mass.: Adams Media, 2010.

LeBoutillier, Nate. *The Ultimate Guide to Pro Baseball Teams.*
Sports Illustrated Kids. Mankato, Minn.: Capstone Press, 2010.

Sports Illustrated Kids. *Full Count: Top 10 Lists of Everything in Baseball.*
New York: Sports Illustrated Kids, 2012

INTERNET SITES

FactHound offers a safe, fun way to find Internet sites
related to this book. All of the sites on FactHound have
been researched by our staff.

Here's all you do:

Visit *www.facthound.com*

Type in this code: 9781476540627

 Check out projects, games and lots more at
www.capstonekids.com

INDEX